I SAW BIGFOOT

BOOK 1

ETHAN HAYES

FREE REIGN

CONTENTS

ONE

SOUTH CAROLINA SIGHTING

SO, I'm not really sure about the exact order of things that happened, but let me know if you think this is weird or not. I never realized what one of these things were until I started listening to your podcast a few years ago. I emailed you a while back, but I didn't share all of my experiences that happened at my childhood home where my mom still lives.

So, I grew up in Marion, SC. It's a tiny town about an hour away from Myrtle Beach. Population's around 6 thousand, and it's spread out. Mom's still out there in the country. Back then, we had two houses on our right, and one across the road from us, opposite a few fields. Country life, you know? To the left and behind our place, there were just fields for miles. Depending on the season, it'd be corn, soybeans, or tobacco. I got two older sisters, and we all lived in this small home with a barn-like thing we called the boat shed. Dad kept his boats, lawnmower, and stuff like that there. In our backyard, we had this big oak tree, and this massive magnolia tree in the front. Funny thing is, mom actually grew up on that land and moved back after she got married and had us.

We used to have these "prowler" issues, as my parents would say. Banging on windows, things going missing from the boat shed, and these "people" peeking into our windows. Now, let me tell you about one time. I was probably around 10 years old, and I had this major fear of the dark – whole different story why – and my big sis asked if I could spend a night in her room. My other sis and I shared bunk beds in another room, and we were super tight, like best buds. Me and the older sis, we had our moments, you know? She could be real mean, but sometimes she'd surprise me with some kindness. Should've been suspicious, really. So, I thought it was cool she was asking me to crash in her room, even though I was kinda scared of her.

Anyway, her room was like pitch black, only light was this red glow from her digital clock on the dresser. So, there we are, in our PJs, and she's telling me to get into bed. This bed's shoved in a corner, so you can only get in from one side. I crawl in, heart already racing 'cause I'm thinking, "What's she up to?" She's being weirdly nice, saying not to be scared, that she'll hold my hand till I fall asleep. I'm thinking she's planning something, like smothering me or something, LOL. So, we're lying there, it's a decently comfy bed, and she kills the light. I'm lying there, feeling better 'cause I can see a bit from the light coming through the blinds. She's like, "It's all good, I'm right here." I'm like, "Fine, whatever." I'm not sure why she's acting so chill, but it's late, and my eyes are getting used to the dark and the tiny bit of light.

I start drifting off, not sure how long I was out, but suddenly, I hear tapping. Even as I type this now, I'm feeling exactly how I felt that night, like 40 years later! I'm just looking around with my eyes, frozen with fear. I don't know why I'm so scared, 'cause I don't know what the sound is. I move my arm under the covers to feel if my sister's there, and yep, she's there, fast asleep. The tapping's coming from the window and it's getting louder and louder. I shift my eyes over, not moving my head, and I see this HUGE dark figure blocking most of the window. I'm holding my breath, feet freezing, realizing that's fear, right? I'm petrified. I think these "prowlers" are trying to break in. The blinds are kinda slanted down, so lying there, I can see a bit of whatever it is. All I can make out is that it's black and has these super white teeth. A big ol' mouthful of 'em, and I can hear it breathing, all raspy and gurgly.

I grab my sister's arm, whisper-shout, "Someone's at the window." She's like, "What?" I say, "Someone's trying to get in!" Trying not to move, talking real low. She shouts, "What?" I scream, "Someone's trying to get in!" She looks, sees the figure, and bolts out of the room, screaming for Dad. I slide out of bed, don't look back 'til I hit the floor, then crawl outta there faster than lightning. "Dad, Dad, someone's trying to get in the window! Hurry!" Now, Mom and Dad are asleep, but Dad jumps up when we scream, grabs his .38 revolver – yeah, he had that thing for dealing with these "prowlers" – and dashes out the front door in his underwear. Mom calls the neighbors, they grab their guns too and go help Dad. Mom's convinced they're gonna accidentally shoot each other, but that's Dad. He comes back in a bit, saying he heard 'em running through the tobacco field, saw a dark figure breaking the stalks, but couldn't see details. And just like that, we're supposed to go back to bed like it's all normal. Yeah, right. I'm in the living room, sis goes back to bed, parents too.

I'm glued to the TV the whole dang night, totally freaked. I can still see it now, like I'm there. Can still hear it. Do I know what that thing was? Nope. But listening to your episodes where people talk about hooded folks or mysterious figures, it all comes rushing back. So, about a year ago, I went back to Mom's. Listened to some more of your guests' stories, talked to Mom – Dad's gone, passed away six years back – but Mom's still holding strong at 84, got my nephew with her, so she's not alone. She's got a load of stories from that house, which I'll share someday. Went back to that window where that "person" was ages ago, measured it up. No bricks or flower beds under there, just the hedges that were always there. The window's bottom is at 5 feet, and that thing took up the whole dang window!

So, I'm guessing it was like 7 and a half, maybe 8 feet tall, unless whoever it was had a ladder or something. Me and Mom just stood there, totally amazed. How did we just think that was a regular person? It hit me like a ton of bricks! Told a few close friends, got the "You're crazy" look and a grin, so I let it be. But I can't. The more I think about all the wild stuff that happened out there, something was going on, man.

TWO
OKLAHOMA SIGHTING

ONE REALLY COLD day in Oklahoma, something totally bizarre happened that I can't forget. You know those days when everything's covered in snow and it's super quiet outside? Well, this was one of those days. The streets were empty, no cars, no people, just this thick layer of snow everywhere.

I was like fifteen and working at this fast-food place about a mile from where all this weird stuff went down. My dad called and said our car was stuck in the driveway because of the snow, so I had to walk home. The snow on the ground was so bright, like reflecting the sunlight.

So, I'm walking, and I see this thing moving on my left. I turn my head and there's this figure playing around in the snow. At first, I thought it was a kid wearing a dark snowsuit or something, but then I got a better look. This thing was covered in long, dark hair or fur, head to toe. And it wasn't a kid, it was like five feet tall and maybe around 160 pounds.

I couldn't believe what I was seeing. This creature was just there, fooling around with the snow, bending over and tossing it up in the air, like it was having fun. But honestly, instead of being excited, I got really scared. I mean, I was pretty far from any houses, and there was nobody else around. It was just me and this strange thing.

I was only about thirty or thirty-five yards away from it, and I had a long way to go before it wouldn't be able to see me. I thought about running, but then I figured if I did, it might start chasing me. I remember reading that animals can do that.

So, I stayed put, just watching it. The longer I looked, the more I realized this wasn't something normal. It was like nothing I'd ever seen before, something out of a movie or something. I kept staring at it, and then I managed to look away and started walking, then running, as fast as I could until I felt like I was really far from there.

Thinking back to that day, it still gives me goose-bumps. It was so strange and scary at the same time. I can't help wondering what that thing was, where it came from, and if anyone else has seen anything like it. It's like a mystery that nobody can figure out, and it's stuck in my mind like a puzzle that I'll never solve.

THREE
NEW MEXICO SIGHTING

HEY, I've got a couple of wild stories that happened out in the mountains of New Mexico, and I can't help but share them. So, here goes – my grandparents used to run this summer camp, nestled about 40 miles east of Albuquerque. Every summer, I'd head out there and basically live the camp life for a while.

Now, picture this – the camp sprawled over this pretty vast piece of land, about 150 acres to be precise, and it cozied right up against the Cibola National Forest. Fast forward to 1992, and I'm 12 years old, just a kid with an adventurous spirit. One day, I'm tagging along with my grandfather, and we're headed to this "power house" to fire up the generator – you know, because we made our own power with a combo of solar, wind, and a backup generator. So, while he's busy tinkering away, I do what I do best – wander off, playing around with the camp dogs. Well, okay, technically they're my grandparents' dogs, but you get what I mean.

Anyway, there I am, having a grand old time with sticks and just doing boy stuff down in a ravine that runs alongside the back of this power house. The sun's on its way down, casting its warm, orangey glow on everything. It's that time of day where it's still kind of light, but you can tell dusk is just around the corner. I'm lost in my own little world when I realize my canine buddies aren't around anymore. That's when I decide to glance up the hillside from where I am, and bam – that's when things get real interesting.

Imagine this – there's this auburn-hued creature moseying across this clearing up the hill. Now, here's the kicker – I can't see its feet, just about knees or thighs up. The sun's playing peek-a-boo behind the hill's crest, back-lighting the scene and making it tough to make out every little detail. But one thing's clear – it's got a human-ish shape, and it's completely covered in hair. It's like nothing I've ever seen before. Smooth as silk, it glides across the clearing in just about three steps. And the head, oh man, that's a whole other story. It's cone-shaped, crowned with these tufts of hair flowing off the back. Now, it's important to note that from my vantage point, I can't see every little thing, like its feet or the finer facial features, but man, the memory of that sighting is etched into my brain.

Now, let me tell you, I'm frozen in place. Petrified is an understatement. My brain's racing, my heart's pounding, and I can't even move a muscle. It's like time stood still. I only see it for a few seconds, but those moments feel like an eternity. It's not until my dogs come back, wagging their tails and tongues hanging out, that I finally manage to snap out of my paralyzed state. At that point, my fear starts to ebb away a bit, 'cause hey, my furry companions are here, right? But truth be told, I couldn't tell if they saw what I saw or if it even fazed them.

Now, I'm back up at the power house, and I've got to tell my grandfather about this. So, I spill the beans, expecting him to be just as wide-eyed as I am. But nope, he's this rational dude, a nuclear physicist no less, and he nonchalantly suggests it was probably a bear. But hold on a sec, I know what bears look like. We had our fair share of black bears in those parts, and this thing I saw? Not a bear. Not by a long shot. The shape, the movement, the color – it all screamed Sasquatch, even though my brain couldn't wrap itself around the reality of it.

Time moves on, as it tends to do, and by the time 2001 rolls around, I've spent countless days hiking and camping on that property. I'm the king of the outdoors, comfortable in the woods like a second home. So, I decide to take on the role of a Big Brother to a ten-year-old kid through a program at my church. We're camping one fine day, just roasting marshmallows by the camp-fire, when the kid's freaked out. He's seen these glowing red eyes across the woods from our tent. I figure it's just a critter, and I go out to check, but there's nothing there. We get back in the tent, but the night's not done with its surprises.

There's this ruckus, this rustling, as if something's building a nest or maybe even a shelter close by. The kid's petrified, and I'm doing my best to calm him down. I keep stepping out, looking around with my flashlight, and every time I do, the noise stops. It's eerie, this weird silence that follows every time I investigate. This back-and-forth goes on for about an hour, until I feel like maybe there's someone out there, messing with us. The thought of a creepy person lurking around gets me more on edge than any wild animal would.

In the end, I lose patience, and I burst out of the tent, screaming at whatever might be out there to scram. But guess what? There's nothing. Not a trace. It's like what-ever it was, it vanished into thin air. We decide to pack up and head back to the house, and as I'm going through the woods the next morning, I stumble upon this bizarre tree structure, not too far from our tent. It's huge, and it's got these claw marks, these long, thin finger marks all around it. It's like nothing I've seen before, and it sets my mind racing.

So, here I am, years later, replaying these stories in

my head. Back then, I didn't think much of it – just chalked it up to weird woodland stuff. But now, as I listen to stories about Sasquatch encounters, the pieces start to fall into place. Those red eyes, the strange structure, the eerie commotion – it's all starting to align. And you know what? Maybe I did come face to face with the elusive creature. Or maybe it's just my imagination running wild. Either way, these experiences, well, they're etched into my memory like some kind of strange, otherworldly campfire tale.

FOUR

PENNSYLVANIA SIGHTING

BACK IN THE DAY, nestled in the rustic heart of York County, Pennsylvania, I had a childhood that was steeped in the beauty of nature and the mysteries of the world around me. Our little piece of heaven was situated near the Susquehanna River, a slice of paradise tucked between the quaint locales of New Bridgeville and Greenbranch. You see, my upbringing was anything but ordinary, for I found myself in the midst of a tale that would make even the most skeptical minds raise an eyebrow.

It was during the fall, a season of vibrant colors and crisp air that invited you to explore the great outdoors. The exact month escapes me, but I remember the warmth in the air, a pleasant reminder that winter hadn't yet tightened its grip. On that fateful day, my two older cousins and I were on a childhood adventure, embracing the freedom of youthful innocence as we roamed the yard and the enchanting woods that bridged our neighboring properties.

Let me give you a glimpse into our world – our home was a little off the beaten path, around four to five miles from the main road. A narrow dirt road, barely wide enough for a single car, meandered through the undulating hills, accompanied by the soothing presence of the Susquehanna River. My mom and I occupied a cozy piece of land, while the wooded expanse between our abode and my uncle's place, my cousin's father, served as a magical pathway connecting our lives. Those woods were our secret realm, a place where our imaginations ran wild as we ventured back and forth, opting for the scenic route over the dusty road. Beyond our land, more woods and the ever-peaceful farm stretched as far as the eye could see.

As the sun dipped lower on the horizon, casting a golden hue over the landscape, the day's adventures began to wind down, and the call for dinner brought us home. Yet, amidst the laughter and shared stories of our day, I realized that something was amiss – I had forgotten a prized possession, some cherished toy or trinket, back by our lawn shed. My mission was clear, and with a sense of purpose, I headed out to retrieve my missing treasure.

The setting sun painted the sky with shades of orange

and pink as I made my way to the shed. A familiar urgency overtook me, and I felt the need to relieve myself, a customary country ritual that required no explanation. However, as I went about this ordinary task, a wave of unease washed over me, an inexplicable sensation that set my heart racing and my muscles freezing in place. It was as though time had come to a standstill, leaving me suspended in a moment that defied all reason.

With every fiber of my being, I felt as if I were being watched, scrutinized by an unseen presence that sent a chill down my spine. Frozen in my tracks, I struggled to comprehend the sensation, my breath coming in slow, deliberate puffs as I strained to pierce the veil of uncertainty that had enveloped me. As I gazed up, I was met with an image that would forever be etched into the tapestry of my memory – a colossal, brownish-red figure, covered in a shaggy coat of fur, gracefully traversing the woods along the edge of the cornfield. It was a sight that defied logic, a being of immense proportions that seemed to belong to another realm entirely.

Fear gripped me like a vice, and though I longed to scream, my voice remained trapped within, stifled by a potent mixture of awe and terror. Before me was a creature of gargantuan proportions, a silent sentinel that exuded an air of majestic mystery. Its body was cloaked in a rugged coat of hair, the strands measuring three to four inches in length, while its elongated arms dangled effortlessly at its sides. Two round, pug-like eyes stared intently at me, captivating and unwavering, as if peering into the depths of my very soul.

The creature's approach was deliberate, a purposeful stride that betrayed an air of quiet confidence. Remarkably, not a single sound accompanied its movement, as if it glided across the earth's canvas with ethereal grace. As my eyes remained fixated on this enigmatic visitor, I couldn't help but note its unusual features – the eyes, round and inquisitive, seemed to harbor a wisdom beyond human comprehension. The jaw was partly open, revealing teeth that gleamed like polished ivory, while the creature's head held an air of curiosity that matched my own.

In the stillness of that fleeting moment, a silent exchange seemed to transpire, a wordless conversation between two souls connected by an inexplicable bond. Time itself seemed to hold its breath as we locked gazes, each seeking to understand the other's presence in this cosmic encounter. And then, as if prompted by an unseen force, the creature emitted a peculiar sound, a gentle huff that resonated through the air. Its head tilted back, those unblinking eyes never leaving mine, while its mouth revealed the gleam of perfectly aligned teeth.

Now, as I reflect upon that surreal experience from the vantage point of adulthood, I recognize the calm that emanated from the creature's demeanor. It bore no sign of hostility or aggression; rather, it exuded an aura of tranquility, as if it sensed that I posed no threat to its realm. Our silent communion continued, a meeting of minds unbound by language, until the world beyond our gaze interjected.

A distant voice shattered the enchantment, a voice I recognized as my mother's urgently calling my name from the front door. The creature, too, appeared startled by the intrusion, swiftly pivoting on its heel and retreating with a grace that defied its colossal form. In a matter of strides, it vanished from sight, leaving behind a sense of wonder and a myriad of questions that would linger for years to come.

As I sprinted back to the haven of my mother's embrace, I found myself grappling for words to convey the inexplicable encounter I had just witnessed. "I SAW A MONSTER!" I blurted out, my breathless utterances met with a mix of concern and skepticism. My mother, ever the voice of reason, dismissed my account as a trick of the imagination, attributing the sighting to the whims of a child's mind.

Weeks turned into months, and the memory of that extraordinary day remained etched in my consciousness. Despite the disbelieving dismissals and the rational explanations, I clung to the truth of my encounter, steadfast in my conviction that I had indeed locked eyes with a creature that defied all rational explanation. Over the years, the memory became a cherished secret, a testament to the mysteries that lie hidden within the fabric of our world.

Now, as a seasoned adult, I find myself recounting this tale with a wistful smile, fully aware of the incredulity it might evoke. Yet, as I listen to stories of Sasquatch and the enigmatic creatures that roam our world's forgotten corners, I can't help but chuckle to myself. If only these storytellers knew the truth that I hold within – a truth that transcends doubt and resonates with the echoes of that unforgettable encounter.

As the years have passed, the memory has only grown more vivid, a beacon of inexplicable wonder that beckons me to the wild places of our world. And though I may never again stand face to face with the enigmatic giant that graced my life that autumn day, the memory serves as a testament to the mysteries that continue to weave their threads through the tapestry of our existence. So, let the skeptics scoff and the doubters dismiss – for I, a humble dweller of York County, have glimpsed the extraordinary, and it is a truth that no rational explanation can ever diminish.

FIVE
TENNESSEE SIGHTING

LIVING HERE IN EAST TENNESSEE, close to the border with Kentucky, has given me some experiences that I still struggle to explain. It's a quiet place, nestled amidst the hills and woods, where my family and I have made a home. Some strange occurrences have left their mark on our lives, and I've often wondered about the mysteries that surround us.

One memory that stands out is when my oldest son recounted an eerie encounter. He had been in the deer blind, that little shelter we set up for hunting, when an inexplicable feeling compelled him to glance out the window. What he saw sent a shiver down his spine – a towering figure with auburn-colored hair, traversing the hayfield above the blind. It was like nothing he had ever seen before, a big, big man covered in hair, disappearing into the distance. That incident left us all questioning the boundaries of our understanding.

Then there's the curious case of the missing eggs. Eggs, you might think, should be a constant in a household like ours, yet they seemed to vanish without a trace. It's almost as if someone, or something, was helping itself to our egg supply, leaving us baffled and wondering. It's a little unsettling, I won't lie, but it's also a mystery we've come to accept as part of our rural life.

One evening, my sons were feeding the chickens a bit later than usual. We have these movable chicken coops that allow us to avoid the hassle of shoveling manure. These sturdy structures sit atop the grass, and on this particular day, they were positioned near a wooded area at the far end of our field. That's when it happened – a bone-chilling scream erupted from the woods, a chilling blend of growl and screech. It was a sound that seemed to pierce the night, sending my sons sprinting back to the safety of our cabin. The source of the scream remained a mystery, its echo leaving us all unnerved.

Our family's journey also led us to building a post and beam strawbale house, a labor of love that consumed our days and nights. I often camped out on-site in a tent, ensuring I was there to greet the sunrise and oversee the construction. It was during one of those nights, in the quiet darkness of July 2013, that I was awakened at 3 AM by an unexplainable impulse. My tent became a cocoon of stillness before it was shattered by a series of screams – loud, human-like screams, repeated five times in quick succession. What was truly astonishing was how rapidly the source of the screams traversed the hillside. The distance it covered in mere seconds left me bewildered, thinking that perhaps someone on a vehicle was responsible. Yet, it moved too fast for a mere human. The ridgeline, the same one my son had seen the enigmatic figure on, seemed to serve as a conduit for this perplexing phenomenon.

The unsettling encounters didn't stop there. During the summer of 2018, as the warm days began to wane, I found myself in a moment of eerie stillness. From the loft window of our temporary cabin, I heard a howl that seemed to defy explanation – it started low, like a deep rumble, before rising in pitch and ending with a coyote-like yip. It echoed through the holler, creating an atmosphere of both intrigue and trepidation. Even my son, in the loft across from me, has his own stories to tell – of fingernails rapping on his window, perched high above the ground. To this day, he keeps a blanket draped over his window, a simple defense against the unknown.

Then came the day I was picking blackberries near the edge of the woods, close to that grove of PawPaw trees. It started innocently enough, with small pebbles being tossed my way. Trying to remain brave, I attempted to keep picking, my heart pounding with each rock that struck the ground near me. In a moment of courage mixed with desperation, I decided to sing aloud, an attempt to quell the rising fear. The tension in the air was palpable, a feeling of being watched and assessed by something unseen. As I filled my bowl with blackberries, I couldn't shake the discomfort that clung to me.

Then, there were the trees. Oh, those massive trees that tumbled down as if pushed by an unseen force. It happened not once, but multiple times – four gigantic trees crashing down while I was out on the farm. The sheer power required to bring those giants to the ground left me awestruck and bewildered, my mind racing to comprehend the inexplicable.

There was also that peculiar night, when I spotted lights in the woods. Our compost heap, nestled beside the apple orchard at the top of the hill, seemed to be at the center of this enigma. My son, perhaps emboldened by a blend of curiosity and naivety, had wolf-whistled into the night. In response, an echoing wolf whistle emerged from the darkness, leaving us both unnerved. Later, as I gazed uphill, I noticed a peculiar phenomenon – a light, a single beam that seemed to stretch from the forest floor to the underside of the leaves. Was it a person with a flashlight? Or was it something else, something far beyond the realm of understanding?

As I reflect on these encounters, I am reminded of the thin veil that separates our ordinary lives from the extraordinary. In a world filled with bright lights and bustling cities, I find solace in the mysteries that unfold under the cover of night, deep within the woods and fields of East Tennessee. It's a reminder that even in our modern age, there are forces and beings that defy explanation, leaving us humbled and intrigued by the uncharted realms that lie just beyond our reach.

SIX
OHIO SIGHTING

GROWING up in a small town out in western Ohio, I was fortunate enough to have grandparents who owned a charming horse farm. Being the eldest grandchild, I had a special bond with my grandpa, and that bond led me on some unforgettable camping adventures from a young age. It all started when I was around 4 years old, tagging along with my grandparents on their camping trips. By the time I was 6, I had already embarked on my first trail ride. Those were the days when we would pack up and head to the great outdoors, exploring places like Hocking Hills, Salt Fork, and Tar Hollow State Park.

Now, let me take you back to a time when the simplicity of life and the wonders of nature filled my days. We may not have had all the modern conveniences at our campsites – no electric, no running water, and no sewer connections. Our campsites were primitive, offering only pit toilets and baths in the creek that meandered alongside the campground. And as if that wasn't enough, my grandpa was adamant about not running the generator for AC, even during the sweltering summer months. Imagine my plight – my bed was perched above the front seats of the RV, a spot that turned into a furnace during those scorching nights. So, if the forecast promised a dry night, my ingenious solution was to sweep out the horse trailer, stack bales of hay, drape them with a tarp, and create a makeshift, cooler sleeping spot right there.

The years from around 1986 to 1994 hold a collection of peculiar memories, events that I used to brush off as odd occurrences with logical explanations. But then, something happened that made me reconsider everything – the moment I first heard the Ohio howl played for me. That eerie sound triggered a memory that was tucked away in the corners of my mind, something I had experienced firsthand.

The setting for one of these curious happenings was the horse camp at Tar Hollow, nestled on the opposite side of the State Park from the main camping and lake area. My routine before bed involved tuning into the one local radio station that came in reliably, just to catch the overnight weather report. Armed with the knowledge of a rain-free night, I would set up my sleeping arrangements for the evening. However, around 1 a.m., my peaceful slumber was interrupted by a strange, yet oddly familiar, sound – it was like a tornado siren, but without the usual pattern. Low to high, then silence for a few minutes, repeating this unsettling sequence about four times over a span of ten minutes. The odd part? The direction from which the sound seemed to originate wasn't where the nearest town was situated. Curiosity got the better of me, and I woke my grandparents up, trying to figure out if there was an emergency. They dismissed it, claiming I must have dreamt it, and sent me back to sleep.

The memories get tangled up between various camping sites, forming a puzzle of experiences that I now recognize as part of a larger, enigmatic tapestry. One such instance took place within the campground at Tar Hollow, where the campsites were arranged in three concentric circles. The biggest circle was situated in the middle, boasting spacious sites for larger rigs. To the south lay a decent-sized circle, while the northern end held a small circle tucked into a heavily wooded area. It was in this small circle that I had an encounter that would forever linger in my mind.

One eerie night, I was roused from my sleep by a sound that resembled a mule's bray. These creatures can make quite an array of odd noises, and given that there was a guy with a mule who occasionally camped nearby, I didn't think much of it. The sound lasted only 2 to 3 seconds, a blend of a scream and a mule's call, emanating from the direction of the small circle. Morning came, and I mentioned this to my grandpa, suggesting that the mule guy had arrived late at night. Our usual morning routine led us through the campground, greeting fellow campers and soaking in the ambiance of the great outdoors. As we wandered back to the small circle, we found no trace of anyone camping there, nor any mules. The eerie memory left me pondering the strange occurrence, especially given the backdrop of a larger narrative that had been circulating around the campfire.

Another camper, a fellow rider who frequented our outings, shared a chilling story that further deepened the sense of mystery. He recounted an incident during one of his solitary rides, accompanied only by his loyal dog. Riding along a familiar trail that we often traversed, he entered a valley that stretched about a mile and a half. There was a smaller valley branching off from this one, ending in swampy terrain and private property. As he rode, he was suddenly struck by a putrid odor, unlike anything he had ever smelled before. His dog darted toward the swampy offshoot, and he heard a commotion as something crashed through the underbrush. The dog returned, covered in a slimy substance that matched the nauseating scent. His tale, however, was met with skepticism, as back then, the concept of Bigfoot was more punchline than possibility. Despite the jabs from fellow campers, he never rode alone again, and the trail that once held routine familiarity was now a path of wary glances and rapid gallops.

Then there was the peculiar incident that transpired on Rattlesnake Ridge, a spot earned its name due to the timber rattlesnakes that frequented the area. The loggers had left a pile of logs and brush near the trail, a spot that served as a haven for these slithery creatures. Our horses, usually prone to a leisurely pace, were suddenly agitated, their nervousness compounded by a putrid stench that hung in the air. It was a smell so foul that it sent us packing after just a few minutes – a rapid retreat from a place where we'd normally rest and recharge. The horses' eagerness to leave struck me as odd, especially given the sweltering heat of the day. The experience led to half-joking comments about Bigfoot's involvement, a topic that had once been a punchline but was now a seed of intrigue.

Our escapades often included a dose of adult beverages, a pleasure that became synonymous with our trail rides. During one memorable outing, a bottle of Wild Turkey made its way into our supplies. By around 1 p.m., one of our female riders had imbibed a bit too much, rendering her unable to ride. Ever the responsible teenager, I volunteered to escort her back to camp. While the rest of the group continued their adventure, we headed back, hoping the fresh air would help her sober up. Guiding her horse at a slow pace, we embarked on the journey back to camp, tackling the familiar trails. But this trip would hold a twist of its own, one that added yet another layer to the mystique.

Our leisurely ride was abruptly interrupted by an overpowering stench that seemed to permeate the air. It was a smell that defied description, causing both of us to wrinkle our noses in disgust. As if the odor weren't enough, our horses were suddenly on edge, hastening their pace as they climbed the hills. Normally, I would rein in my horse during such ascents, but their urgency overruled my control. By the time we reached the crest, the horses were heaving, and a sense of unease settled over the surroundings. The source of the odor remained a mystery, as we couldn't find anything amiss in the vicinity. Ultimately, we made it back to camp without any further disturbances, but the incident left an indelible mark on my memory.

Perhaps the most spine-tingling encounter, however, unfolded within the confines of my sleeping quarters – the RV trailer. It all began with an odd rustling sound, like someone gingerly treading through the creek located about 30 yards behind the trailer. Now, the creek was no walk in the park, its bed composed of flat sandstone that could rival a skating rink. Yet, there it was – step, pause, step, pause – the distinct cadence of footsteps echoing through the night. Just as I puzzled over this phenomenon, another peculiar sound joined the nocturnal symphony – the clacking of rocks, arranged in groups of three. Clack-clack-clack, followed by a pause of two or three minutes, only to repeat the eerie pattern five or six times. As I tried to make sense of it all, the puzzle pieces slipped into place when I heard our horses growing restless and nickering.

The sound of our horses, which were tethered between the trailer and the creek, filled the night air. It wasn't an unusual occurrence on its own, but coupled with the otherworldly sounds from the creek, a sense of foreboding crept over me. I peered into the darkness, straining to discern any movement or shape in the night. My gaze followed the horses' line of sight, their focus directed toward a particular spot. Yet, despite my efforts, I couldn't spot anything unusual. I shrugged it off, chalking it up to a curious deer or some other animal wandering through the woods. Exhausted and wary, I tried to settle back into slumber, hoping that the myste- rious disturbance was nothing more than a fleeting anomaly.

These fragments of my past, woven together, create a patchwork of enigmatic experiences that defy simple explanations. They transport me back to a time when the mysteries of the natural world sparked my curiosity and left me contemplating the unknown. As I recall these memories now, I'm reminded that the world is a vast and intricate tapestry, and sometimes, within the ordinary fabric of life, there are threads of wonder and inexplicable phenomena waiting to be unraveled.

SEVEN
OKLAHOMA SIGHTING

IN THE WINTER OF 1989, when I was a teenager, I had a sighting on the reservation. I was 15 at the time and saw a tall, hairy man rapidly crossing the road during a snowstorm. He was huge, and the whole thing happened so fast that it was hard to get a good view. I reported it to the tribal government, and they took my statement. I was always curious about what I saw, and that sighting has led me to work for the tribal government in Oklahoma now.

Over the last ten years with the tribal government, I was the one assigned to investigate any reports of a large creature on the reservation. Occasionally a report would come in and I would investigate it, but for the most part the reports of a hairy creature stopped. About a year ago, I began taking in more reports from people who were seeing a large figure they described as a Sasquatch, with demonic eyes. They believed these sightings were a bad sign or warning. Recently, one of my co-workers said his mother saw something near their house, which is in an area with lots of trees. The description was almost identical to what I saw as a teenager. He said that the large figure is "hanging around" near their home. She doesn't live on the reservation but just outside of town.

I had mentioned to my boss that I saw something like that when I was a teen. He sent me to spend a night or two just south of the reservation in the wilderness to investigate since I had a previous encounter. I went to the nearest wooded area that had camping, found a spot, and set up my tent. A creek was nearby as well. There were also large areas of evergreen trees nearby where any large animal could easily hide.

I made it to the campsite early in the afternoon and set up. I also had a few trail cams that looked like rocks, so I spread them around the area in hopes of catching something on video.

It got dark quickly, and I decided to go to sleep early since I'd most likely be up in the middle of the night. I had only been asleep for about 2 hours when I heard something hit the side of my jeep, like a rock. I dismissed it, but then I heard it again.

I came out of the tent and looked around the area with my flashlight. On the passenger side of the jeep, the side that was facing away from my tent, I found a few dents in the door. I knew they weren't there before. I looked on the ground and saw a bunch of rocks. It looked like someone had been throwing rocks at my jeep. Unfortunately, the trail cams weren't facing that way. When I returned to my tent, I noticed that the front of the ten had been slashed. It looked like it was slashed by a large claw.

I slept lightly and through the night I could hear a type of grunting which was followed by a bizarre yell and other sounds. I woke up around dawn and decided to go and check the trail cams and see what had happened while I slept. I grabbed my bear spray, flash-light, and my rifle and headed into the woods.

Unfortunately, the trail cams had not been tripped so there were no recordings of what was making the yells and screams in the night. I noticed markings on the tree trunks that looked like claw marks, like the marks that were inflicted on my tent. Some of them were fresh and I do not remember seeing these on my preliminary walk through the afternoon before.

As I continued to look around, I noticed there were no sounds of birds and small animals. There were several strange shaped and bent small trees, almost twisted in two. I know I did not see them the day before either. I felt in my gut I should go back to camp, but I was curious, and I kept going. It only took about ten minutes before I started to hear a low-pitched growl. I reached in my pocket for the bear spray, to just be safe. I never saw any evidence of a black bear or of Sasquatch and decided to check along the creek.

The creek wasn't too far from where I had camped the night before. There were not a lot of trees along the creek bed. I thought I might have an easier time looking for any tracks or other evidence that would indicate what was out here. When I got to the creek, I walked down the edge near the water. There were a few dead fish on the banks. It looked like something pulled them out of the water and ate them fresh, then just left the bones. I walked a little further and then I started to smell a very foul and rancid odor, like something was rotting and then a little worse. I thought there might be partially consumed fish or other animals around, but I was unable to find anything or the source of the odor.

I continued to walk down the creek and kept my eyes open for any signs or activities of bears. There were not any, but I did stumble upon another pile of half consumed fish. I looked around and closer to the water, where the ground was still soft. I found a series of large footprints. The prints led from the water and up to the pile of rotting fish. At best guess, the prints were made by a creature who was walking upright. The print was about 17 or 18 inches long and about 6 inches wide. There was a well-defined heel and what appeared to be four toes. The top of the prints was a bit smudge due to the mud, but it appeared to be a bipedal animal. I had my camera with me and took several photos, one which included my foot for a size comparison. I was unable to find any more evidence along the creek, so I returned to my camp.

Seeing as how my tent had been ripped open the night before, I decided to pack it up and head back into the office.

EIGHT

TENNESSEE SIGHTING

I WORKED on a farm in Western Tennessee and on the weekends, I worked in town at a second job. I live just outside of Ridgely. Since I worked 7 days a week, I never had a problem sleeping, until this one night in October of 1999. I just couldn't sleep.

It was around 1:00 AM. I decided to get up and go into the kitchen and get a glass of water. I stood at the kitchen sink, and I started to stare out the window. It was dark in the back - we didn't have any exterior lights at that time. The area surrounding my house is mainly wooded and my house was situated below a sizable mountain. Inside, there were a few small kitchen lights that were plugged into the outlets near the floor for safety. The weather was good that week. There was no rain or wind that night.

Out in the backyard, I noticed three pairs of red eyes

walking in single file. They were about 20 yards away and in the woods at the back of the yard. I grew up here and had hunted my entire life. I knew all the animals that were local to the area. I had seen all types of animals and eyes walking around in my yard at night before, but not like this. Something felt different this time.

These eyes were different from other animals. They were up higher, around 7 feet from the ground. That ruled out any local wildlife I could think of. The eyes walking through the woods were intense and were glowing a red color. They were the same red as a "Coke Cola" bottle-cap. I noticed that these eyes stayed at the same height - there was no bounce in their steps. Whatever was walking around was most likely heavy and had a very smooth stride. Even though it was pitch-black outside, I could only see a few moving branches in the yard. I didn't see any figures or silhouettes. I did not hear any noises or vocalizations.

Directly behind my house, there were about four miles of wilderness. It was mostly government land, and I was never sure what they did with it. It just remained untouched and stayed that way, almost like it was a buffer zone between the houses and the facility. I wasn't sure what I saw walking around back there. I originally thought that it was a Sasquatch or some other unknown creature. I had heard for years about people seeing things on the government land and we joked that they were doing some sort of hybrid experiments. I never told anyone that I saw something there that night. It was a small town, and I didn't want word to get around and have people start to think that I was seeing things, or I was delusional.

The next morning after the "bottle-cap" incident, I woke up early and walked over to the spot where the eyes vanished deeper into the woods. I looked around and I found a fresh tree branch that looked like it was snapped off from the tree. I looked up and about 9 feet up you could see where the branch used to be. It appeared like something huge had just twisted it and snapped it off. It was large and about 4 to 5 inches in diameter. I didn't check for tracks because of the ground cover. There were a lot of fallen leaves and twigs on the ground already and it would take too long to look for any type of tracks. While I was walking around, I did stumble across an area that had a peculiar smell. I could tell that it was barely lingering on. It smelled like maybe there was a group of rabid skunks that were there and then were frightened, sprayed the trees, and then disappeared.

I walked around for a little bit more and I tried to climb up to where I saw the eyes disappear. It had started to get too difficult for me to climb to where I lost sight of the eyes, even though whatever I saw out here had moved easily across the land and through the trees the night before. I think one thing that kept me from getting to sleep was the neighbor's dog. It had started barking around 11:30 PM and continued for an hour.

About a week before this happened, I woke up in the middle of the night by strange noises outside. My neighbor's dog was barking that night too. It sounded what I imagined a tree being hit with a baseball bat or pipe would sound like. There was a pattern to it too. Three knocks, silence, then three more knocks. That kept going for about half an hour. There was silence for a little bit, and I started to go back to sleep, but then there was a huge sound of metal being smashed. This went on until about 3 AM.

The only other person who heard all the banging was my sister who was visiting with her two children. The kids slept through it, but the next morning my sister asked what all the ruckus was about the night before. I have not heard of any other Sasquatch reports like that.

NINE
COLORADO SIGHTING

I WAS ten years old when my mother met the man who would become my stepfather. We lived in Illinois, and he lived in Colorado. They met online in one of those old chat rooms from the nineties when the internet first started becoming a thing. Though they were together for more than a year when my siblings and I finally met him and when my mother finally met him in person, it wasn't until we were all packed up and moving to Colorado to live with him that I would meet him face to face. His name is Stan, and he was a nice guy. I tried to be stubborn and hold onto my anger over my mother moving us so far away from my dad and the only home we had ever known but Stan was a good guy and my siblings, and I couldn't help but warm up to him. Stan had a cabin in the middle of nowhere and while my siblings and I felt very out of place there, having grown up our whole lives in Chicago, we quickly acclimated to the solitude and peace the forest that surrounded us brought. I have four siblings. I have one younger sister and three older brothers. We had to drive a few miles to get onto the main road in the tiny town the cabin and forest were in, to get the bus to school. We had no neighbors, but we all had so much fun, and Stan taught us everything he knew about living in the woods. By the time we had been there a year it was like we had lived there our whole lives. One of the main things he taught us was how to detect and protect ourselves, if necessary, from wild animals. There were a lot of predators in those woods, but we hardly ever saw any of them and when we did, they would stay away from us if we stayed away from them. It was a really great time in our lives.

One night, after we had been there for a little over a year, my mom and Stan went out on a date. They were going to be gone all afternoon and wouldn't be home until after it got dark outside. We weren't nervous or anything and when they left my siblings and I decided to go play manhunt in the woods. We all had walkie talkies and it was something we did often. We weren't afraid to be in the woods in the dark, but it was summertime and therefore we had plenty of time before the sun went down. We all went and played the game and had a good time. My little sister always tagged along with me because I was the closest to her in age and honestly, I was the nicest of all of us boys to her. She looked up to me, I guess. As we were looking for a good hiding spot, my sister stopped suddenly in her tracks and told me she felt funny. She said she thought our brothers had already found us and that we should hide somewhere else. When I asked her why she thought that she said that she felt like we were being watched and had heard a funny noise. I stopped to listen for a minute and the same feelings of being watched overtook me. It was overwhelming and for some reason I felt a strong sense of fear and dread as well that seemed to have come out of nowhere. I also heard what sounded like someone walking, because there was rustling in the leaves somewhere nearby. I didn't see anyone though and there were no animals around either. The forest didn't go quiet, but it went very still. It was eerie suddenly and I couldn't put my finger on why. My little sister started to cry and said she wanted to go home. I radioed my brothers, and they came and me up with us. I offered to bring her home and stay with her, but it seems the feelings and emotions she and I had been feeling were contagious and all my brothers felt it too. We just wanted to get out of the woods.

We talked about it amongst ourselves as we walked and decided it was because only a day earlier Stan had told us some stories about a local legend, and something he saw with his own eyes a few times in those same woods, about a wild man. That's what he called it anyway. He said it was a gigantic ape-like creature, but it wasn't an ape at all but a man. He claimed it was primitive and had come from long ago, when the area started to be more populated, and some of the human beings went to join the new settlers and some chose to remain in the woods, living off the land and remaining "wild." It was quite a story and it sounded so ridiculous and obviously made up, none of us took it very seriously. We were suddenly starting to rethink our initial assessment of those tales. However, Stan was also a prankster and we all had that in the back of our minds. That's when we heard the first growl. It was low and guttural, and it didn't sound like any of the animals we had all become so familiar with. We looked around but didn't see anything. We started walking faster. We heard another growl and what sounded like something was banging on the trees around us. My oldest brother screamed that the wild man was out there, and he and my other two brothers took off like lightning through the woods, leaving me and my sister out there to fend for ourselves. My little sister screamed and started crying hysterically so I picked her up and started to run after them. I took one more look around as I did so and that's when I saw the hairy creature.

It was at least ten feet tall. It looked like the incredible hulk in a gorilla suit, but it also had the face of a man, but not quite. It really did sort of look like modern depictions of cavemen. I ran with all my might and almost caught up with my brothers as the beast chased us through the woods. We were all screaming and terrified and the faster we ran it seemed the faster it became, and it gained on us very quickly and easily. We all made it to the cabin at around the same time, but my brothers got in the door first and they locked me out! I was pounding on the door and screaming for them to let us in, but they wouldn't. They said the wild man would come in with us and me and our little sister should go hide somewhere else. I almost couldn't believe it. To make a long story short I grabbed her and ran to the open garage and put her in the old car Stan had in there that he had been working on as a hobby with one of my older brothers. I then proceeded to run as fast as I could to the door to close it, just as it was closed almost all the way, I heard a loud growl and saw the wild man's feet. It slammed into and banged on the metal garage door. I crawled into the car in the front seat and got down on the floor. I told my sister in the back to do the same. Five minutes later we didn't hear anything anymore and I got out of the car to be able to listen better. The door to the house that was connected to the garage swung open suddenly and my brothers told me and my sister to get inside. For the next hour I yelled and screamed at them, crying the whole time, wondering how they could just lock us out and leave us to the mercy of that creature the way they had. They made no apologies though and eventually we all settled down. It was eight o'clock before we knew it and the sun had gone down. We all decided to stay in our mom and Stan's room with all the lights off until they got home. Our little sister fell asleep on their bed while the four of us just sat there quietly. None of us wanted to say it but we were all scared that thing would come back and get us somehow if we made any noise. We knew it was lurking out there somewhere, just waiting for the right moment to strike.

I went to the window to look outside and see if I could see the headlights to my mom's car coming up the hill that led to our driveway. I kid you not, the second I put my face to the window, I was greeted with a hideous face staring back at me. I was looking in the eyes of the wild man. I screamed and immediately started to cry. My brothers all looked and saw it too. For it to be even with the window the way it was it had to have been eleven feet or more. It took up the entire window too. It was massive and it was mad. It wanted to get us. We thought we had gotten away but now there was nothing but a piece of glass separating it from us. We all ran to stand against the door, which was as far away from the window that we could get without leaving the room. The beast put its first right through the window as if it were nothing and it seemed like it didn't faze it one little bit. It roared and the stench coming from it was overwhelming. We could do nothing but stand there and scream, even as we heard a loud crashing sound coming from the kitchen, which was the room right behind the door we were standing up against. There was more than one! It took a moment for that to really register. We didn't know what to do and the one at the window was trying to climb in. It was vicious and its face was twisted in rage and determination. It wanted to get to us, and nothing was going to stop it. We heard loud banging and all sorts of random noises coming from the kitchen and we knew another one was out there and that it had smashed the glass of the back door. Suddenly and without warning, the noises in the kitchen stopped and the one in front of us trying to get through the window stopped what it was doing as well. It looked like it was listening and finally and for the first time, its attention was drawn away from us by something. It took off running like a bat out of hell and when my older brother went to the window, he said he saw three of them, all of them as big or bigger than the one trying to get into the bedroom, running faster than he ever saw anything run in his life, back into the woods. I heard my mother scream for us.

We all ran to her. We came barreling out the front door and me and my little sister tried jumping into her arms. We were terrified and traumatized. All my mother and Stan saw though was the dents in the closed garage door. We were all yelling and talking over one another, but Stan seemed to pick up what we were saying immediately. "The wild man?" he said, "you saw him?" We all said that we did, and he ordered all of us kids and my mother inside the house immediately. They saw the mess and my mother was about to throw a fit because she thought that we had broken all the glass and made the mess. Stan understood and told us all to go to our rooms. He and my mother fought for hours about the fact that he had never told her about the creature. She knew how dangerous it was and how it could have ended very tragically. Eventually life went back to normal, but it was never the same again. We had a lot of long-term effects and eventually myself and two of my brothers were diagnosed with post-traumatic stress disorder because of what we had been through. We were hardly ever left alone in the cabin anymore and when we were, it was only when it was necessary, and we were left with a gun. We all had to learn how to use several different types of firearms too. I never saw the creatures again, but I know now that they were what everyone refers to as bigfoot. They weren't friendly and they weren't full of peace, love, and rainbows. They were dangerous predators who surely would have killed every single one of us had the car not scared them off that night. I think they followed us home and remembered where we lived. They were cold and calculated and I'll never forget the anger, the rage in that thing's eyes as it stared us down trying to get to us through the bedroom window. We invaded their territory, and they got revenge by invading ours.

I've often wondered if what Stan told us about where they came from and what they are is true. The eyes were cold, but they looked very human, despite the hatred in them. We didn't play in the woods much after that and we all moved as far away from there as we could without abandoning our mother and Stan, as soon as we were old enough to go out on our own. This tale should serve as a warning for anyone who has any fantasies in their head about what bigfoot is and how they behave. It could be the difference between life and death, whether you heed this message. Thanks for letting me share it.

TEN
MONTANA SIGHTING

IN THE SUMMER OF 2001, I was working in Monarch, Montana as an animal control officer. The department kept getting complaints forwarded to us about a dumpster near the edge of town being tampered with. Residents were finding garbage taken out of dumpsters and then thrown on the ground.

After several weeks of reports, I decided the only way to find out what was doing this was to go out at 3 AM to see if I could catch the 'culprits' in action. I thought I would find either humans or raccoons going through the trash dumpsters. I went to the area in question, turned off the truck and headlights and rolled my window down. I was within five feet of the dumpster. I was there about 30 minutes before any activity happened.

While sitting in my truck, I saw the large silhouette of a human-shaped figure. I waited for a bit and the figure started to open the dumpster and began to throw trash around and on the ground. I quickly turned on the headlights so I could catch him in action. As soon as I turned the headlights on, I saw an extremely tall figure completely covered in hair and going through the dumpster.

The figure was about seven feet tall and was covered in dark, brownish-black hair. The hair was shaggy too and I noticed the hair was thinner on the arms. The arms hung low and seemed like they started basically at the base of the head. They hung down past its knees. I really didn't see much of a neck, but it had broad shoulders and a large oval-shaped head. I could see the eyes. They were totally black. It had hair on its face, but not around its eyes or mouth. As soon as my headlights hit the figure, it looked at me like it was scared.

Right away it started moving off. It didn't run but walked real fast in a weird jumping-skipping strut. Not like a person would run. I think I saw it for about thirty seconds before I got my truck in reverse and got out of there. While I was backing up, I did notice this really bad odor. It was like a wet dog smell mixed with rotten eggs, sulfur, and sewer overflow. It's one of those smells you just can't ever forget. I watched as the creature disappeared into the shadows and I just couldn't believe it. I had seen Bigfoot in the recycling bin.

A few weeks later, in August, my sister and I were

driving down State Rd 89, just past Monarch. It was early evening. The sky was starting to get darker than it normally should have been, and I knew there was a storm approaching. It was still enough light to see without headlights. Just after I passed a golf course, the road took a turn into a heavily wooded section. There was something on the road that caught my eyes.

Crossing in front of me, about thirty yards away, were four figures walking across the road. They were walking single file, heading east from one densest part of the woods to the other side where it was also very dense. My sister and I both gasped at the same time. I recognized that tall, hairy figure from that night a few weeks ago. It was Bigfoot again.

The first one in the line was the largest and was about eight feet tall. It was covered in the same dark brownish-black hair as the one I saw near the dumpster. Behind him was a slightly smaller figure, which I assumed to be a female. Then there was a smaller creature. It was about six feet tall. I assumed that to be a younger Bigfoot. There was also a fourth creature following. The smallest one was between four to five feet tall. They were all holding hands and walking single file. They didn't seem to be in that much of a hurry. They all had long legs and they all had long strides, so I know they could have moved faster if they wanted to. I think they were going slower so the smaller one at the back could keep up. The family of

Bigfoots walking past us didn't seem to care that we were close and in my truck. I rolled down the windows to hear if there were any sounds or vocalizations. There were no unusual noises or sounds, no grunting or talking. Even the birds were silent in the trees as the Bigfoot family passed through. They simply walked past us and back into the woods. Since there was a huge storm on the horizon, I thought they might be trying to get somewhere and take shelter. I knew there were a few wild caves that way and I thought they might be heading there.

I wanted to wait to see if there were any more Bigfoots who were hurrying and looking for shelter, but the storm was almost here, and my sister really wanted to get home before it hit. On the way back to Monarch, I told my sister about the reports we had been getting about someone breaking into trash bins and about the creature I saw that night.

PUBLISHER'S EXCERPT

WHAT LURKS BEYOND

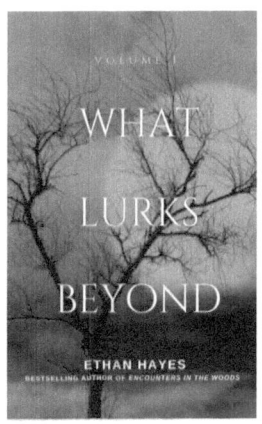

THE DEVIL'S HOUSE

Growing up in rural Alabama in the seventies didn't leave me with much to do as far as entertainment was concerned. When I was twelve years old my friend and I were bored and looking for some excitement. We got a lot more than we bargained for and what happened to us that day is branded into my memory and my nightmares as though it happened only yesterday. It all started one weekend when my friend Phil was staying at my house. We were fifteen years old. I had one older brother who was intent on making my life a living hell and unfortunately he was also having friends stay over that same weekend. I knew he was going to go out of his way to be a jerk to me and Phil but there was nothing that I could do. He was eighteen years old and much bigger than us. His friends were just as big jerks as he was and Phil and I were planning on being out of the house as much as possible while he was there. It was the middle of summer and the weather was fairly cool considering how hot it normally got in that area at the time.

Friday night came and Phil came over at around six o'clock and had dinner with me and my family. My brother and his jerk friends were there and picked on us the whole time. My mother tried to get them to stop and my father, who Phil took after more than my mom, thought it was hilarious. He tried not to show it though. Jerks! After dinner Phil and I just went into my room and hung out. We watched some television and then decided to go to bed around midnight. We stayed up talking for a while though and eventually the conversation ended up on the old, abandoned house behind my house. There were woods behind my house and they were very dense and right on the edge of the other side there was a house that everyone in the neighborhood avoided because it was said to be haunted. No one had lived there as far as I knew, since at least when I was born. I had asked my mother about it and she told me that there was some sort of tragedy or other that happened to an elderly couple that lived there. Of course she said that the haunting stories were all just rumors. Rumor or not they were pretty terrifying to me as a kid. There was said to be the spirit of the old woman who died there, who was also said to have been a witch depending on whose story you believed. The old witch woman was believed to have put a curse on the land and whoever dared enter either the house itself or even just the property was said to end up cursed as well. There was another rumor which said that you could possibly end up being attacked by her or worse, killed. It was believable to us at the time, remember we were only fifteen years old. The kicker is that some of those rumors ended up being exactly the truth and right on the money.

I don't remember which one of us came up with the next bright idea but it was discussed that we should maybe go and explore the house and the property surrounding it the next day. It was only something we kicked around in our heads before falling to sleep and we had not made a set decision on it before we both fell out. I had nightmares that night about the house and the property surrounding it. Though I'm sure now that the house was owned by someone, I had no idea who that someone was. There weren't any caretakers and the whole property was overgrown with weeds and other undesirable things which made the whole, giant old Victorian look even more sinister, even during the daytime. My nightmares consisted of being chased around the house and out into the woods but not by a witch. I was being chased by giant shadow beings and somehow I knew if they caught me I would end up dead or somewhere else- somewhere much worse than where I believed I would go when I died. I jumped up in a cold sweat, relieved that they had only been nightmares. The next morning Phil confessed that he had had the same type of nightmares but I didn't tell him I had them too.

We were all having breakfast in the kitchen when my brother started his stuff again. The constant picking on and teasing us was really getting under my skin and my mother wasn't able to really do anything to stop it. Phil and I decided to go out for the day and find something else to do. We ended up just riding our bicycles around the neighborhood and spent some time at another friend's house. We were supposed to be back at my house before it got dark but we were having so much fun that I called my mom and asked if we could stay out a little longer. She agreed and gave us some more time.

Within the hour Phil and I were headed back to my house. We were walking our bikes and it was dark outside. We were trying to decide if we wanted to walk through the woods and take the shortcut or if we just wanted to stick to the main roads when we suddenly found ourselves right in front of the house from our nightmares. We had our bikes with us but it was such a nice night we didn't feel like riding them. Phil looked at me and smiled and I knew immediately what he was thinking. He wanted to go in. However, I was wrong- sort of- because he then dared me to go in. He said he would wait outside as a look out because it was private property and no one was supposed to be trespassing as there were several signs all over the place that told us as much. I refused to go in alone and after several minutes of us going back and forth, we both walked our bikes into the huge front gates and parked them where they wouldn't be seen from the street or the road. We both were going to go in and see what all the fuss was about. Aside from all of the horror stories surrounding this old house, it was interesting to me to finally be able to see what it looked like on the inside. Plus, I had been afraid of and avoiding this house my entire life, this would be my chance to squash all of those seemingly silly fears. To be honest, we were both thinking of having bragging rights, too because no one we knew had ever actually gone inside before.

The front door was all boarded up but there was a broken basement window that we were both able to fit through. I just happened to have had my backpack with me, because I carried it everywhere during the summer. I had allergies and other health issues and had to take medication at specific times throughout the day, every-day. There were two small flashlights in there because we were always trekking through the shortcut in the woods at night and we both had lighters on us because we had just started experimenting with smoking. We had the flashlights on before we went through the window and figured we would use the lighters for backup. The place reeked to high heaven like urine and feces, that's the very first thing we noticed. There were spider webs everywhere and probably rats as well. This place was the epitome of a haunted house in a horror movie. It was dusty and moldy and gross. We paid careful attention to where we were walking because we had entered through the window in the basement and there were four floors above us that we planned on exploring. From the moment we went through that window though there was an ominous feeling that came over the both of us. We both knew and sensed something was wrong but we both chalked it up to being a little nervous about finally being in this house. We found the stairs and went up them together. They were loose and rickety and every-thing you would expect from the type of house I've been describing to you so far. The house was even bigger on the inside and we first wandered throughout the downstairs. We heard a noise like someone moving furniture around coming from directly above us. While every instinct in my body and everything about the situation was telling me to run, I was thinking of my brother finding out and never letting me live it down. I was half smiling despite my fear knowing that now I had one up on him because I knew for a fact that he had never been brave enough to enter this house. Phil heard the noise too and we both jumped at the same time.

Neither one of us would've ever admitted we were scared and neither of us would have ever admitted defeat before the other one. We were best friends but we were also teenage boys. We went up the next flight of stairs to the second floor and looked around. All we had were the dying beams of light coming from our dainty little flashlights and they were illuminating less and less the longer we kept them on. At that point we just figured that it was an animal or something knocking things over but once we got up there and started looking around a little bit we quickly realized there was nothing there that could have been making that noise. In fact, there wasn't anything at all in any of the rooms. The house was completely empty of furniture altogether and while there was dirt and debris all over the place, nothing that could be mistaken for furniture being dragged or moved across the floor was anywhere in sight. My heart was pounding and I suggested to Phil that maybe we should just leave. He quickly agreed and we turned to walk out of the room. The door slammed shut in front of us and our flashlights died at the same exact time. We both screamed and didn't care if the other one heard it. I quickly went into my pocket and grabbed the lighter but when I finally got my shaking hands to get it to light, it quickly was blown out. Seriously, something was blowing it out. There was absolutely no wind outside and at first I thought that it was Phil and that perhaps he was breathing heavily. I mean, I could hear him breathing heavily and so I yelled at him to back up. He asked what I meant and where I was. His voice was coming from all the way across the room. Something else had blown out my lighter. I ran to where I remembered the door to be and tried to open it but it was locked. I didn't know how this was possible because we were inside of the room and I didn't remember seeing any sort of lock on the outside of the door. Who puts locks on the outside of bedroom doors? We were trapped in the room.

I yelled for Phil and he responded that he was there. There was a little bit of light coming in from the street through the two small windows in the room and I could see him over by the one window trying to get it open. The streetlights were out in front of the house so when I say there was a little bit of light I mean just that.

Suddenly I saw something move out of the corner of my eye and froze. It was a massive shadow figure. I know now that that's what it was and it looked just like it had in my nightmares the night before. I called for Phil but he was in such a panic and trying to get the window open that he didn't seem to hear me. This thing was dark and solid enough that I could see it clearly despite being in a dark and almost completely lightless room. It was slowly going directly towards Phil. It had the overall and general shape of a person and looked like it was wearing some sort of cloak or hood. I couldn't tell if it was walking or floating but it was moving fairly slowly. I once again yelled for Phil as it dawned on me that this thing was most likely about to try to push him out the window. He heard me and when he turned around it seemed like he immediately saw the figure. I don't know where he got the courage or presence of mind to be able to think as quickly as he did and he immediately went over to the other window and threw the flashlight through it. By this point the shadow entity had all but disappeared and while I could still feel its presence, I could no longer see it anywhere. Phil said he was going to jump. It wasn't a very far fall but there was the risk of breaking or spraining an ankle. At that point though, I figured it was better than being trapped in a room with this huge and hulking shadow being. I couldn't decide if it was better to not be able to see it or if it would have been better to keep my eyes on it. I honestly don't know and still can't figure out where it went or why it had made itself unable to be seen anymore.

The energy in the room felt like pure evil. I know that may not make much sense to many people reading this but if you've ever been in a similar situation or in the presence of one of these cloaked and shadowy figures, you probably will understand what I'm talking about. Phil took his chances with the jump and I followed right behind him. We landed hard but neither one of us got any serious injuries from it. Phil immediately started running towards the woods, to the shortcut to my house. I turned and looked up at the window we had just broken and jumped from and saw the shadow being standing there, just watching me. I ran after Phil. We left our bikes there and of course my parents asked where they were. We were forced to tell them and they weren't happy at all. In fact, they took us to pick up the bikes and drove Phil home right after. He wasn't allowed to stay the night again as we had originally planned. My parents didn't believe us about the shadow being and told us that we had to pay for the window. They tried to find out who owned the place but they never could and I still don't know. My brother was impressed when he heard what Phil and I had done, and from that day on he let up a little bit on the teasing and picking on us. I haven't had another supernatural or paranormal experience since but

I don't need to in order to believe in it all. I remember that day so vividly and even sitting here typing this gives me the chills and the creeps. I wouldn't wish such terror on anyone.

———

WHAT LURKS BEYOND, VOLUME 1

ELEVEN
ONTARIO SIGHTING

ALRIGHT, let me share this wild story that happened not too far from where I live, up in the Hastings Highlands area, near Lake St. Peter, Ontario. I've been camping at the same park there for about 30 years, and let me tell you, I've seen my fair share of moose, bears, deer, wolves, birds – you name it. But what I'm about to tell you, it ain't any of those usual suspects.

So, there's this spot locals call the "dump," where folks go to chuck their garbage and stuff. It's also the place where tourists and campers sneak in to try and catch a glimpse of black bears. It's so common that you'll find loads of vehicles there, with people watching these bears. Well, one evening, I decided to take my buddy along, he's from Toronto and never seen a bear before. We set up and waited, 'cause usually when there's incoming traffic, it spooks the bears, and then you wait for 'em to reappear – takes about half an hour on a busy night.

Now, this particular night, the dump had set a few fires to manage the garbage piles. So, I told my buddy the chances of spotting any bears were rare 'cause they're wary of fire. After waiting for about half an hour, I told him it wasn't our night and he was a bit disappointed, but he understood. And right then, when we were starting to pack it in, we saw this huge log fly through the air from one corner of the lot, followed by raccoons and critters scampering out like crazy. We're both looking at each other like, "What the heck?" Then comes this incredibly loud, bone-chilling scream or growl that just sent shivers down our spines.

Now, through all the smoke and the light from the fires, we notice the outline of a person there. We're thinking, "Is that a ranger or a worker?" We kinda shrugged it off, but then we turned on our headlights. As soon as we did, this thing jumped down into a hole full of garbage, and we could still see its head sticking out.

Mind you, this hole is like 10 feet deep. We were scared out of our wits, so we start the vehicle and inch forward a bit. Just then, this thing screams again, turns towards us, and hurls this massive appliance right at us. It jumps out of the hole and starts challenging us. We're both terrified, can't believe what's happening. It's easily 10 feet tall, massive, and grunting at us. We decide to hightail it out of there, but as we're leaving, we see it in the rearview mirror until it fades away.

So, we reach the entrance, stop, and get out – even though my buddy's against it 'cause he's scared out of his wits. I light up a cigarette and try to wrap my head around it all. And then, out of nowhere, BAM! A rock smashes into my windshield. (Yeah, I've still got that windshield, can show it to you.) And then comes this terrifying scream. We could hear this thing approaching, all the cracking and thumping getting closer. We freak out and bolt out of there.

I drop my buddy off back at the campsite, get him settled down, and we agree to keep it to ourselves. Still scared but super intrigued, I tell my dad. He's up for it and wants to check it out. I'm freaked, but I take him along since the dump is just a quick two-minute drive from the campsite. We drive back, pull in, and just as we're reaching the end of the winding road that leads to the dump, this huge creature sprints across the road. It's like 50 feet wide, and it cleared it in just a few strides – that's enough for my dad. He saw it, and we turn right around and head out.

Oh, but here's the kicker. Later that night, we all hear the dogs from the post office/general store going absolutely berserk. Their barking and commotion could be heard all the way from our campground. We thought maybe wolves were attacking the dogs, but then, at the end of all that noise, we hear that unmistakable scream. It spooked everyone, and while it wasn't super loud due to the distance, it was unique enough to send chills down everyone's spine. The next morning, the campground owner tells us that five dogs had been attacked, and guess what – they were missing! Broken chains, signs of a struggle, but no dogs.

Okay, so that's the long story. Sorry for rambling, but I've never done this before. I've got all the nitty-gritty details and a lot more to tell about this Sasquatch encounter, but this area, right around where those Halliburton tunnels are, from that other caller you had? Yeah, that's where it happened. I've been coming here for three decades, and I truly believe that this whole Algonquin to Toronto stretch of woods is a squatch hotspot. I mean, it's so densely forested, like that other caller said, you can't just stroll through it – you can't even see through it. I'm telling you, these creatures are out here, and they're out here in numbers.

TWELVE
NEW HAMPSHIRE SIGHTING

HEY, I'm from New Hampshire, and after reading some books, including yours, and hearing about other people's encounters, I finally feel brave enough to share my own experiences. Seriously, what I've seen is just mind-boggling.

Okay, so my first run-in happened back in 6th grade – I'm in college now, just so you know. At that time, I was really into playing travel football around the Northeast, which meant early mornings and some travel. I've grown up in New Hampshire, so I've seen my fair share of regular Northeast animals like deer, black bears, and foxes. I mean, it's nothing out of the ordinary. Now, this particular morning, I was getting ready to head to a tournament in Massachusetts, which meant an early start – like 4:30 or 5 in the morning. As I was eating my cereal, I noticed something odd through my sliding glass door.

See, I've got a view into my neighbor's backyard through some trees, and when the leaves have fallen off, you can easily see his place from my dining room table.

So, there I am, munching on cereal, when I spot this decently sized deer in my neighbor's yard. Now, we've got some pretty good-sized deer here in NH, so it's not a shock to see one. I glance back at my cereal bowl, and out of the corner of my eye, I catch a blur of movement. Before I know it, I'm looking up, and that deer is down on the ground, with this massive, bulky figure crouched over it. It's like this giant dude, as if one of the world's strongest men threw on a ghillie suit and decided to take down a deer. The sheer size of him was mind-blowing.

I stared at him for a few seconds – not too long – and then he looks up from the deer, just like I had glanced up from my cereal, and locks eyes with me. Now, the view wasn't crystal clear because of the trees and branches, but one thing was for sure: he knew exactly where I was. And I had a gut feeling that the distance between us could be covered real quick. If he decided to make a move, that glass door wasn't going to do much to stop him. We held this gaze for what felt like forever, but was probably just a few moments. Then, he reaches down with his massive arms, picks up that deer like it's a piece of paper, and looks right at me. I'm no expert on deer or humans, but considering how hefty that deer was and how much it must've weighed, I find it pretty darn hard to believe that even the toughest strongmen could lift it up so effortlessly, just tuck it under their arm, and walk away.

So, I'm tracking this guy's movements with my eyes, and when he stands up, I realize he's incredibly tall. I mean, he's not just the thickest and widest "human" I've ever seen – he's also the tallest, by a long shot. And here he is, right in my state, in my neighbor's backyard. It doesn't make any sense – nothing about that creature added up. The speed, the strength, the size – none of it made sense.

Now, onto my second encounter. This one happened a few years later when I went camping up North with an ex-girlfriend. We were up in a state park way up in northern NH. We arrived pretty late at night, and the campground was quite rugged – the kind that experienced campers like. To be honest, we didn't really care about that; we just wanted some alone time, you know, typical stupid teenager stuff. So, we set up our tent late, and I gotta say, things didn't feel quite right to me. I mean, I knew there were other people around, but it felt like they were keeping an eye on us.

We get the tent set up, do our thing for a while, and then I had to hit the bathroom. There's this outhouse with showers a few hundred feet from our site, so I grab my little flashlight and head over. As I'm walking, I notice there's not another soul around us. That feeling of being watched was getting to me, but I tried to brush it off. Then, I hear some snapping sounds to my left, up on this little hill. I turn to look, and peeking out from behind this boulder on the hill is this massive figure. I could only see part of its head and shoulder, and they were both incredibly thick. This thing pops out for a split second and then disappears behind the boulder again. I didn't hear it leave immediately, but trust me, I wasn't about to go up there and find out.

To be honest, I was shocked I didn't wet myself right then and there. I did what I needed to do and then high-tailed it back to our campsite. I never told my ex about it 'cause she was super jumpy about anything supernatural. But let me tell you, that incident left me on edge for the rest of that camping trip.

THIRTEEN

OHIO SIGHTING

LET me take you back to my junior year of high school in 2012. Picture this – Morgan County, Ohio, an old gas road snaking through Wayne National Forest. It was one of those evenings in mid to late April, that hint of spring in the air. I was out there on a mission – Turkey scouting was the game. You see, the turkeys roosted in that neck of the woods, and I had heard their calls many times. So there I was, on the cusp of darkness, trying to communicate with the turkeys using a couple of hoot owl sounds. But there was silence. Not even a peep.

I paused for a moment, just sitting there, and then I heard it – shuffling down the trail a little ways ahead. My initial thought was that I'd startled a deer or maybe a couple of raccoons. These woods were known for their critters, after all.

Determined to get some action, I took a few steps

down the trail, maybe a couple of hundred feet or so. I had a plan – I wanted to hoot again, see if I could get a turkey gobble in response. That would have been a solid confirmation that a Tom would be roosting near that tree come morning.

But then it hit me – a putrid, gut-wrenching stench. It was a smell that had me thinking of death, like a rotting carcass. I followed my nose and went over a hill, half-expecting to come across a dead deer. It wasn't deer season at that point, but there had been some issues with what they called blue tongue or something similar. It made me think that maybe a deer had succumbed to it.

So, I peered over the hill, scanning the area. But there was nothing there. Well, not exactly nothing. Movement caught my eye – there was a large oak tree, and behind it was a head. A big head, mind you – blackish brown and staring right at me.

Now, here's where it gets wild. My first thought, believe it or not, was "gorilla." Before you dismiss that, let me explain. You might recall the Zanesville exotic animal massacre. Over 50 exotic animals were set free by their owner, who tragically ended his own life. The local authorities had to take down these animals – think bears, lions, cheetahs, tigers, even wolves. So, the idea of a rogue gorilla wasn't entirely outlandish in my mind. I mean, this was just a couple of miles from my house, and a mere 49 minutes from Zanesville, Ohio.

Curiosity got the best of me, so I took a cautious step closer. As I did, the creature – let's call it that for now – pulled itself partly from behind the tree. What I saw then was staggering – it was crouching, yet still towering over me. I'd estimate it stood somewhere between 6 feet 6 inches and 7 feet tall. A true giant in the animal kingdom.

Then, in an instant, it changed the game. The creature burst into a sprint, coming right at me. Adrenaline surged through me, and my instincts kicked in. I braced myself, lowered my shoulder, and dropped my head. With a guttural yell that I won't repeat here, I prepared for impact. I locked eyes with the creature when it was maybe 15 feet away – a moment frozen in time.

But fate had other plans. At the last possible moment, the creature seemed to veer off, pivoting in a different direction. Maybe my scream had startled it, or perhaps it simply changed its mind. I didn't wait around to find out. My heart pounding, I turned and bolted, racing back the way I came.

When I got home, I shared my heart-pounding experience with my stepdad. His response? Laughter. He'd hunted those woods for years and had never seen or heard anything remotely like what I described. But I knew what I saw, and the memory stuck with me.

I've ventured back into those woods since that day, searching for a trace of the enigmatic creature. Yet, like a phantom, it seemed to have vanished without a trace. Perhaps these creatures are like bears, capable of roaming several miles. Maybe it wasn't from the immediate area and had just wandered into that patch of forest.

Whatever it was, one thing's for certain – that encounter was etched into my memory. The Ohio woods hold mysteries beyond what we can fathom, and to this day, I can't shake the image of that towering, crouching figure, a true enigma of the wild.

FOURTEEN

CALIFORNIA SIGHTING

LET me take you back to the summer of 1980, a time when I was just a 10-year-old kid exploring the wilds of Trinity County, California. My dad was living in a quaint little town called Hayfork, nestled amidst the rugged landscape of tall trees, shrubs, and open land. He had a cozy haven on a 10-acre patch a few miles up the mountain, at the end of a dead-end road. It was a time before smartphones and video games, and I was excited to be spending the summer there with my dad, his girlfriend, her two kids, and my brother – a mix of teenagers and me, the young explorer.

The cabin my dad had built became our haven. It was a rugged structure with planked floors, a grand wood stove, and a split log sofa that must have seemed like the pinnacle of comfort in those days. The summer heat had us kids raring for adventure, and we decided a sleepover outside would be the perfect way to experience the wilderness. Gathering our gear, we set ourselves up under the starry night sky. It was a seemingly innocent idea, until the eerie hour of midnight when my resolve wavered. Suddenly, the idea of sleeping outdoors lost its charm, and I decided I'd rather head back to the cabin.

The neighbor boy – my newfound friend – offered to walk me part of the way home. The moon cast a soft glow, painting the road with its light as we meandered down their driveway, flanked by tall, imposing trees. Eventually, he pointed me toward the gate in the distance – our cabin was just a stone's throw beyond that point. My unease began to grow as I contemplated that final stretch, but I didn't want to appear scared.

As he disappeared into his own driveway, I began my solitary walk to the cabin. The plan was simple: reach the gate and then sprint like my life depended on it, straight to the safety of the cabin. The latch clicked shut behind me, and as I turned around, my heart skipped a beat. Roughly 100 feet away, something caught my attention – a figure, a presence, moving through the clearing. My mind raced, desperately trying to make sense of what my eyes were taking in. It was a figure that resembled a man, I told myself, running alongside a dog-like, wolfish creature. Fear surged through me, freezing me in place.

Nearby, a massive manzanita bush seemed to beckon me, offering me cover. I crouched down and hid, watching, waiting. Time seemed to stretch, each moment an eternity as the figure continued its dash toward the thicket of trees. Finally, it was gone from my line of sight. The adrenaline coursing through my veins propelled me forward, and I sprinted to the cabin, my heart pounding in my chest. I collapsed onto the rustic split log sofa, my head sinking into a well-worn, dirty pillow. It might have been uncomfortable, but it was a sanctuary – a haven. Beneath me, I could hear the faint sounds of rodents scurrying beneath the floorboards, but I felt safer than I had ever felt before.

Inexplicably, I chose to keep my harrowing experience to myself. Looking back, I can't quite understand why. Maybe I wasn't even sure what I had seen. The memory lay dormant for years, a secret locked away. It wasn't until recently, much later in life, that I started to openly share my encounter. And that's where your podcast came into play – discovering it was like finding a key that unlocked a door I had long forgotten.

The creature that had dashed through my vision left me bewildered. It didn't fit neatly into any box. The best way I can describe it is as a lean, tall being – maybe a Bigfoot, maybe not. The moonlight offered enough illumination for me to make out its general form, and it's an image I can still summon when I close my eyes. The thing that puzzled me even more was the dog-like creature beside it. I've wracked my brain trying to come up with an explanation, but the pieces just don't fit neatly together.

The gate was a portal between worlds, between safety and the unknown. The creature's movements were otherworldly, a blend of grace and peculiarity. It moved differently – legs that seemed to navigate uneven terrain, arms that scooped in an almost rhythmic motion. The details might have been shrouded by moonlight, but the impression it left on me was indelible. I can't say with certainty that I came face to face with a Bigfoot that night, but I can say with absolute certainty that it wasn't an ordinary man walking a dog. The mysteries of that summer night remain, a vivid memory etched into the fabric of my past.

FIFTEEN
TEXAS SIGHTING

IT WAS the late spring of 1985 and El Paso, TX was the backdrop for a bewildering encounter that etched itself into the memories of myself, my brother, and two close friends. The stage was set with a dramatic late afternoon thunderstorm that lingered longer than usual, unleashing a deluge of rainwater that transformed the neighborhood's stormwater retention basin into a sight to behold. This reservoir, typically mundane, was now a glistening expanse, a testament to the storm's power.

As evening descended, my brother and I embarked on a bike ride to our friend Jimmy's place, with a pit stop at Tom's house en route. The camaraderie was palpable as we pedaled through the neighborhood. Our destination was set – another friend's house – but fate had other plans for us. Drawn by curiosity, we found ourselves at the basin's edge, awe-struck by the sheer volume of water that had accumulated there. It was a scene none of us had witnessed before, and the allure of this unusual sight compelled us to pause and take it in.

The clock had struck ten, casting the surroundings in an inky darkness. The feeble glow of a distant streetlight barely managed to cast a pale aura on the basin's water-line. As we stood by the street curb, gazing across the waterlogged expanse, a peculiar sight arrested our attention. A figure materialized on the far side of the basin, partially illuminated by the faint porch lights of the nearby houses. Our initial assumption was that it was a person – after all, what else could it be?

With intrigue tinged with a hint of jest, one of my friends dared to call out to the enigmatic figure, "We see you over there!" But there was no response. The figure remained stationary, its unsettling swaying movements casting a mystifying air over the situation. Like a pendulum, it shifted left and right, up and down. Our attempts to make sense of this odd behavior only deepened the puzzle.

Playfully, my friend Jimmy added a hint of bravado to the mix, shouting, "We're coming over there to kick your ass!" This proclamation, seemingly innocuous, spurred the figure into action. It began to move, a dance of sorts, a pas de deux with itself, tracing a curious pattern along the water's edge. It swayed, it shifted, and it defied explanation. Our collective bewilderment grew.

Then, as if caught in a bewildering illusion, our gaze momentarily wavered. And in that fleeting lapse, the figure vanished. Panic surged through us, and our focus shifted to the right side of the basin, the direction from which the figure had vanished. Dark shadows seemed to weave a tapestry of mystery, and our flashlights, feeble beacons of light, struggled to pierce the shroud.

Suddenly, a sound – the gentle, rhythmic shush of water being displaced – drew our attention to the heart of the basin. Instinctively, I swung my flashlight downward, casting a dim illumination on a series of delicate ripples, a serenade of liquid motion moving toward me. It was as if the water itself held a secret, whispering tales of the enigma that approached.

My gaze followed the course of the ripples, tracing their path upward until they converged on a sight that would forever be etched into my mind's eye. Before me stood a figure – an embodiment of the inexplicable. My flashlight's beam first danced upon its chest and two arms, shrouded in a coat of light brown hair. The chest itself was a lighter hue, akin to a sun-kissed tan. As I lifted my gaze, the figure's head emerged from the darkness, and in that pivotal moment, our flashlight beams converged.

Two beams of light met the figure's gaze, and the world seemed to hold its breath. Eye shine, an unearthly green-gold brilliance, stared back at us, an unspoken testament to the unknown. Time stood still, the world reduced to that surreal tableau – two beams of light and a pair of mesmerizing eyes. And then, in a heartbeat, adrenaline surged through my veins, propelling me onto my bike, my senses aflame with primal urgency.

My brother, my friends – we were a swift-moving tide, racing back to Jimmy's house as though the very essence of the unknown pursued us. Bikes clattered, heartbeats thundered, and we sought refuge within the safety of Jimmy's garage, the door sliding shut behind us. There, beneath the dim glow of a single bulb, we regaled Jimmy's mother with our astonishing tale. Our words tumbled out in a frenzied rush, fueled by the sheer bewilderment of what we had witnessed.

Her calm demeanor and understanding gaze soothed our frenetic nerves, though her reaction was far from the panic we felt. She listened, her motherly wisdom serving as a balm for our shared experience. As we recounted our encounter, our voices echoed the enigma that had unfolded under the cover of night.

Hours slipped by as we hashed and rehashed the details, dissecting every nuance and attempting to unravel the mysteries of that fateful evening. The events that had unfolded defied explanation, remaining lodged within our collective consciousness, a puzzle without a solution.

Though time has moved on and years have passed,

the memory of that encounter remains as vivid as the day it transpired. The memory of the swaying figure, the mesmerizing eye shine, and the inexplicable dance between light and shadow continues to linger, etched into the annals of our shared history. And while the years may have dulled the edge of uncertainty, the essence of that encounter remains – an enduring enigma, a chapter in the chronicles of the unexplained.

SIXTEEN
MISSOURI SIGHTING

SO, back in 2018, during my construction project days, I had this wild experience that I just can't forget. Now, you gotta know, I come from Wyoming, a place where the Bighorn Mountains were like a second home to me. Nature and the great outdoors were in my blood. But after moving to Missouri and getting into the construction gig, I found myself traveling all over the state for my work. That's when things took a seriously unexpected turn.

It was a typical morning, around 5:30 AM, and I was hitting the road with one of my crew members. We were headed to a job site about 3.5 hours away. The sun was barely up, and the world was just starting to wake. As we were driving along, something out of the ordinary caught my eye. It was this big, dark figure that sort of stepped out from the trees onto the road. My first thought? Bear, of course. But this bear was different. It was standing on two legs, which is pretty weird for a bear. I started easing off the gas to get a better look.

As I got closer, I realized this wasn't your usual bear behavior. It was moving, well, kind of gracefully. Like it was gliding across the road. I mean, bears don't move like that, right? And the steps it was taking, they were huge. In just two steps, it crossed the entire two-lane highway. I was gobsmacked, to say the least. But then things got even weirder. As I passed by, it stood up taller, turning toward my car. I caught a glimpse of its head, and that's when I knew something was really off. It definitely wasn't a bear. My gut was telling me, "Bigfoot."

I know it sounds crazy, but that was honestly what crossed my mind. Bigfoot, the legendary creature people talk about. I couldn't believe it. I had to turn around, to see if I could spot it again. I was itching to get a better look. So, we doubled back. But guess what? By the time we got back to where I saw it, it had vanished. Just like that. Vanished into thin air.

Now, here's where it gets even more bizarre. While we were parked there, scratching our heads, another car came zipping up the road from the opposite direction. They slammed on their brakes, came to a screeching halt, and then sped away like they were fleeing from something. I kid you not, it was like a scene from a thriller movie. That moment right there, it sent shivers down my spine.

And you know what made it even eerier? The whole area got deathly quiet during that sighting. No birds chirping, no rustling leaves, nothing. It was like nature itself was holding its breath. I can't even begin to describe how unsettling that silence was. I mean, I've been in intense situations before, being a former marine and all that, but this was a whole different kind of unnerving.

So, we hit the road again, heading to our destination, but my mind was just racing. What had I just seen? A creature that was walking on two legs, with a head that wasn't like any bear I'd ever seen. I kept replaying the whole thing in my head, trying to make sense of it. But honestly, to this day, I still can't explain it. It's one of those things that sticks with you, you know? A bizarre encounter that makes you question what's really out there in the woods.

SEVENTEEN
COLORADO SIGHTING

I RAISED my kids in the same cabin in the mountains that I grew up in. It's an old miner's cabin in the middle of nowhere and completely secluded from everything and everyone. It's located in Colorado, and it takes anywhere from forty-five minutes to an hour just to get down the mountain and back to any semblance of civilization. The closest big city is two hours away and the tiny town at the bottom of the mountain is another forty-five minutes to an hour once you are down that mountain. I bring all of this up just to enforce how secluded our home really was, but we wouldn't have had it any other way. Growing up, and my kids have always said they've felt the same way, it was like living in a fairytale. The moose, bears and other wildlife were our only neighbors and my kids played together in those woods and all over our gorgeous property without any fear, just as me and my siblings had done. My encounter with the strange and possibly paranormal didn't happen until all my kids were older and moved out of the house except one. My daughter had moved back in with me. My wife, her mother, had passed away suddenly a couple years before and I had a bad accident one night when it snowed on the mountain, and I was caught in it trying to get up the mountain. I was driving much too fast and ended up driving off a cliff. Luckily, I got away with only two torn rotator cuffs and a broken hip. It took me a long time to convalesce from those injuries and my daughter Jaime was the only one of my kids who wasn't married yet. She didn't have as many responsibilities as her older siblings and so she moved back into the cabin to help take care of me. It was a very long and painful recovery process but by the time the end of Spring rolled around I was feeling a lot better and a lot like my old self again. My daughter had been a Godsend and I don't know what I would have done without her. One night she and I were sitting in the living room, each of us reading a book, when there was a loud banging sound that made us both jump.

It sounded like it was coming from the side of the cabin. My immediate thought was that someone was trying to break in but immediately that didn't make sense because if it were someone trying to burgle us, they would have been trying to get in through the front door or one of the windows. The banging was coming from the side of the house and neither one of us could understand it at all. I went into my bedroom and grabbed two guns. I handed one to my daughter and told her the minute she saw someone coming through the door or one of the windows to just start shooting. The whole cabin was shaking and while I briefly considered that maybe it was a confused moose that was ramming the side of the cabin, that also didn't make much sense once I put some thought behind it. Whatever was banging on the side and slamming into it, had hands. I don't know how we both knew that, but we did, and we were sure that it couldn't have been an animal. However, the banging had so much force behind it we were also sure that it wasn't a human being either. I honestly thought the logs were going to come rolling into the house, that's how bad and violent it was. There were other noises too, that gave away the fact that it couldn't have been a human being. The growling and heavy breathing weren't noises humans typically made. Whatever it was sounded extremely angry though and it also seemed intent on getting inside of the house. We turned off all the lights and just waited. We stayed like that for almost an hour before it stopped, and we didn't hear or feel anything anymore. I ran to the window and peeked out, but I didn't see anything out there. We were both very scared but as a father, I tried to downplay my fear and the situation itself, to try and make my daughter not only feel better, but much more comfortable. She was terrified and I hated to see her feeling like that in her own home.

I calmed her down after about twenty minutes of reassuring her that it had to have just been a confused moose and eventually, we both went to bed. A week passed without any other strange or scary incidents, and I felt like I was finally ready to get out of the house. I had been cooped up all winter and aside from staying on the property, I hadn't been outside that whole time. I hadn't been able to do any of the things I loved all of which involved being in the woods. I wanted to start off slow so I asked Jaime if she would accompany me on a walk. We had always gone for walks and while her siblings and my wife would accompany us sometimes, it was something Jaime and I enjoyed doing, just the two of us, since she was very small. We had a trail that we called our own and she immediately agreed to go with me. I had to take it slow and to get to the head of the trail we had to drive down the mountain just a little bit. I let her drive and we parked off to the side, where there was a space for someone to park but I think that was for emergencies or something, back when the mines were open and running for the miners who lived all over the mountain in the cabins, and not for leisure activities. However, we figured it didn't matter much because ours was the only cabin still standing and even if someone did call the authorities and complain, their fastest arrival time would have been two hours. We didn't plan on being out there for that long anyway. I took my time and Jaime stayed right next to me the whole time. Jaime had a backpack with her with bear spray and a blow horn in it. I had taught my kids to respect the wildlife out in that forest and on that mountain from the time they could walk. We've been on many walks and hikes out there where we ran into a mountain lion or hungry bear and all we would have to do to get them to quickly run away and leave us alone was to sound the blow horn. They would be so terrified they would leave us alone very quickly. I was proud of her for remembering because I hadn't thought of it. I've often wondered if that's what saved our lives that day. I won't ever know for sure, but I have a suspicion that it just might be.

We walked for an hour and were just about to turn back when my hip really started hurting me. I had to stop for a few minutes and take a break. I could see Jaime was worried about me, but I reassured her I was okay. The truth of the matter was that, while I was in pain, a very strange and unusual feeling was coming over me as well. I felt scared but there was no apparent reason for the fear I was feeling. The hairs on the back of my neck stood up suddenly and I noticed that it seemed like there was no noise anymore throughout the entire forest. Just as I thought about how quiet and eerie the usually very inviting and comfortable woods were, my daughter spoke up and told me she was experiencing all those same things. I told her not to be silly, that everything was just fine and that we would make our way back to the car in just a minute. It was going to be dusk soon and no matter how safe we always felt out there we both knew that being out there in the middle of the forest on the mountains in the dark was simply inviting trouble or an animal attack. I saw something moving out of the corner of my eye. I didn't look right away because I didn't want Jaime to follow my gaze. I somehow just instinctively knew that something was watching us from over to the right side of me. I casually glanced over there and sure enough I saw something. I couldn't make out exactly what I was looking at because it was far enough away that all I could make out was that something was there. The shape of it didn't look familiar as it was far too tall and wide to have been a human being but for those same reasons it couldn't have been an animal either. I was even more frightened at that point and so I decided to play through the pain so to speak and told her we needed to start walking back to the car and that we needed to do it quickly.

She didn't ask any questions and we were on our way. We had only been walking for five minutes or so when I looked down and saw about a hundred shell casings. They were all over the ground and scattered in all different directions. It occurred to me and the first thought that popped into my mind was that someone else had been out there, and that they had been forced to defend themselves against something using one hundred rounds of ammunition. I couldn't even fathom the creature that it would take that much ammunition to stop an attack from. I could tell Jaime was thinking the same things as I was but before either of us could say a word, we smelled the most horrible, rotten smell we had ever come across. It made our noses burn and our eyes water. I knew that whatever I had seen watching us when we were taking that short break was still out there, that it was still watching and now following us and that it had been whatever the person had been shooting at. I told her to move quickly, and she did. Suddenly a giant rock whizzed past Jaime's head. She turned around and at first, she was giggling because she thought I was playing some sort of joke on her. She had been in front of me and when she turned to look at me, she realized immediately that it hadn't been me who threw the large, softball sized rock at her. I had two torn rotator cuffs and though they were healing, I couldn't throw a pebble with either arm. I saw the figure step out from behind some trees about a yard away from where me and my daughter were standing. It had black hair all over its body, was eleven feet tall and half as wide or more and it looked evil. It just seemed malevolent somehow and I heard the words in my head "get out of here and don't come back" but I can't be sure if the creature was communicating with me or if I just had enough common sense to know we needed to hustle. I told her to keep walking and not to look anywhere but at the ground. It looked like a giant, black ape and it was pissed. We had encroached upon its territory.

As we walked, we heard growling sounds, extremely loud ones and I knew the creature was right behind us. We heard it crashing through the woods and those same softball sized rocks were whizzing past both of our heads as we got out of there as fast as we could. The more we walked the closer the growling and breathing sounds got to us and I knew we were going to be attacked. I knew it was about to make its move, we were moving too quickly for it not to attack us, and that it was about to do it soon. I told Jaime to stop and hand me the blow horn and when she did, I squeezed it and it blared through the woods. I did that four or five times and it seemed like it backed the creature off. I didn't see it anymore and neither one of us heard it. It wasn't until we got to the car that we heard a very loud and ferocious sounding howl/growl that echoed through the woods and made my blood run cold. As we got into the car, I took one quick look back and saw the creature standing there, arms crossed over its chest, staring at us with hatred in its eyes. We drove home. Once we got to the cabin, we locked all the doors and windows and slept in the living room that night, with one of us on each couch. We haven't had another issue or encounter with whatever that ape-like creature was in the woods, and it's been eleven years. However, we are much more careful when we go on walks now, and Jaime always makes sure she isn't out there at night under any circumstances. I walk with my grandkids now and my kids and Jaime and I have both told them the story of what happened to us out there. It took months for us to put two and two together that the creature in the woods was more than likely the same one that had been trying to bust through the logs to get to us inside of the cabin the night before.

I didn't know what to make of all of it at first but Jaime and I, after doing some extensive research online, are more than satisfied that what we encountered that day and the creature trying to break into the cabin, was bigfoot. I know many people believe that bigfoot is peaceful and just wants to be left alone, with some of them even going so far as to believe they are spiritual beings from other dimensions. While all of that may be well, good, and true in their experiences, in mine and Jaime's we knew we were going to be killed. I wholeheartedly believe if I hadn't thought to blow that airhorn that day that would have been the end of us. While it didn't completely get rid of the bigfoot creature, it did slow it down and make it hesitate enough that we were able to make it back to our car and get the hell out of there.

EIGHTEEN
ILLINOIS SIGHTING

BACK IN THE mid-90s I was out in Rosedale, Illinois, just minding my own business, picking up creek stones for my wife's flower bed. You know how it is, just going about your day, not expecting anything out of the ordinary.

This stretch of Rosedale Valley is about 2 to 3 miles long. There's this road, Coon Creek Road, that winds through it, with a creek on one side. And then, on the other side, there's this open field that stretches up to the hillside. Both sides of the valley are these thick woods, and the terrain can get pretty steep.

I had been down there by the creek, tossing those stones up by the road. I must've walked about a mile and a half down that creek, and I was on my way back to the van. And that's when things got weird. It's like all of a sudden, my senses were on high alert, and the hair on the back of my neck stood up. Have you ever had that feeling, like something's not quite right?

Anyway, I stopped in my tracks, just looking around, trying to figure out what set off my instincts. And then, I saw it – this massive, dark thing on the hillside across the field. At first, I thought it might be a tree stump or something, but there was something off about it. It was this dark brown to dusty gray color, and it was swaying from side to side, real slow.

I couldn't take my eyes off it, like I was in a trance or something. And then, out of nowhere, it stood up. I mean, picture this – this tall figure, like 7 to 8 feet, covered in hair, just standing there. And the weirdest part? The more we stared at each other, the more that swaying got intense. It was like some kind of standoff, and I was locked in this silent conversation with whatever this thing was.

But you know how it goes, right? Reality finally snapped back, and I was booking it back to the van. Adrenaline pumping, heart racing, the whole nine yards. And as I was sprinting, I could see this creature, whatever it was, starting to make its way up that steep hillside. Now, that's no easy feat, my friend. But it was like it knew I was spooked and was just showing off.

The crazy part is, as it was climbing, it turned around and looked back at me one more time. Like it wanted to make sure I was getting a good view of its disappearing act. I mean, can you imagine? It's the kind of thing that makes you question reality, you know?

I've shared this story with folks, and I've gotten my fair share of reactions – some laughs, some raised eyebrows. But let me tell you, when you lock eyes with something that's way out of the ordinary, it sticks with you. And that swaying, hair-covered mystery on that hillside? Well, it's a memory that's gonna stay with me for a long, long time.

NINETEEN

ARKANSAS SIGHTING

IN 2022 I had an encounter with what I think was a bigfoot on the Buffalo River in Arkansas. I'm out there hiking the bluff trail, or as they call it, the goat trail. I'm all about capturing some awesome photos and just enjoying the great outdoors. Now, I'm not one to usually chat about this kinda stuff, but there's always been this inkling in me that there's more to the wilderness than meets the eye.

So, I park my truck at the steel creek campgrounds, a spot I know from a previous adventure with my son. The trail follows the river, crossing it a bunch of times. Armed with my trusty camera, I set off early in the morning, around 7:45 or 8. I cross a couple of creeks, take some snapshots of the water and those towering bluffs. All seems well and peaceful.

Then things start getting eerie. I'm about a mile into

the hike, and I've just finished my second creek crossing. Now, I'm walking into an area with tall grass and trees, and that's when I hear it – this deep, guttural sigh or grunt. My heart's going haywire, and then it happens – this massive creature stands up right in front of me.

I can't see it clearly, just catch a glimpse of the back of its head and this absolutely colossal hand brushing a tree branch aside as if it's no big deal. The trees around it are swaying and creaking as it moves away, and all I can do is stand there, feeling like I'm stuck in some surreal dream.

Honestly, I'm frozen solid, except for the fact that I didn't end up wetting myself, which I can only credit to my pre-hike bathroom break. But let me tell you, my legs might as well have been glued to the ground. It's like time's suspended, and there I am, watching this scene that defies all logic.

Eventually, I manage to shake off the shock. I figure, "Okay, pal, you can either freak out and flee like a headless chicken, or you can keep your cool and just continue what you came here to do." So, I choose the latter, but I decide I'm gonna make as much noise as humanly possible. I start chattering away to myself, just so that whatever that was knows I'm still very much present.

I proceed to the bluff, snap some pics, and try my best to act nonchalant, even though my mind is racing a mile a minute. A few hours later, I'm heading back to the same spot, and then I hear it – this massive crash that sounds like a tree being ripped apart. I turn my gaze, and I see the trees shaking, but it's not heading toward me, it's like they're swaying in the direction that creature had gone.

Instinctively, I whip out my phone to capture the moment, hit record, and – you guessed it – everything suddenly stops. No more trees moving, nothing! It's as if whatever it was sensed the camera and thought, "Nah, I'm outta here." By this point, I'm practically shouting every thought that pops into my head, cause I'm rattled, to say the least. Armed with nothing but my voice, I dash back to my truck like there's no tomorrow.

I can say that I wasn't really terrified in the sense that I'll never go back out to the woods alone. In fact I've been back over a dozen times since and haven't seen or heard a thing, but one day I'm sure I'll run into it again.

———

CONTINUE WITH
I SAW BIGFOOT, VOLUME 2

ABOUT THE AUTHOR

Ethan Hayes grew up in Oklahoma and moved to Texas when he attended Texas A&M. Upon graduation he was hired by Texas Parks and Wildlife and remained there until he retired twenty-two years later. He currently lives in southeast Texas with his wife and two dogs. When he's not spending time enjoying the outdoors and writing, he sips a cold beer on his front porch while listening to Bluegrass music.

————

Send in your encounter story:
encountersbigfoot@gmail.com

ALSO BY ETHAN HAYES

ALSO BY FREE REIGN PUBLISHING

STAT: CRAZY MEDICAL STORIES

MYSTERIES IN THE DARK